S0-AIS-386

BUILDING CHRISTIAN CHARACTER

CASEY
THE GREEDY YOUNG
COWBOY

A BOOK ABOUT
BEING THANKFUL

442

Michael P. Waite
Illustrated by Anthony DeRosa

Chariot Books
David C. Cook Publishing Co.

First Baptist Church
MEDIA LIBRARY

For my buckaroo niece, Shawn. *MPW*

To Barbara. *AJD*

Chariot Books is an imprint of David C. Cook Publishing Co.
David C. Cook Publishing Co., Elgin, Illinois 60120
David C. Cook Publishing Co., Weston, Ontario
CASEY THE GREEDY YOUNG COWBOY
© 1988 by Michael P. Waite for text and illustrations

All rights reserved. Except for brief excerpts for review purposes, no part of this book may be reproduced or used in any form without written permission from the publisher.

Cover design by Dawn Lauck
First printing, 1988
Printed in the United States of America
93 92 91   5 4 3 2
Library of Congress Cataloging-in-Publication Data
Waite, Michael P.
      Casey the Greedy Young Cowboy
      (Building Christian character series)
      Summary: A young boy, who wants his parents to buy him more cowboy equipment, learns a lesson about thankfulness when he meets a rodeo star who has no family. Includes a related Bible verse.
      [1. Gratitude—Fiction. 2. Greed—Fiction. 3. Christian life—Fiction. 4. Stories in rhyme] I. DeRosa, Anthony, ill. II. Title. III. Series: Waite, Michael P. Building Christian character series.
      PZ8.3.W136Cas 1988   [E]   87-35512
      ISBN 1-55513-615-X

Dear Mom and Dad,

Did you ever hide your child's pill in a spoonful of jelly? That's how the lesson about being thankful for what you have is tucked into *Casey the Greedy Young Cowboy.* The teaching is couched in a fun, rhyming story.

You and your children can't help but smile at Casey and his "need" for more cowboy paraphernalia. But there's no missing his message: Be thankful for what you have.

How can you use this book to help train your children?

Read *Casey the Greedy Young Cowboy* aloud, as a family. Talk about the story and why being thankful is important for God's children. Discuss Psalm 118:1, the verse found on page 31, and memorize it together. The verse will serve as a reminder of the Christian character trait of being thankful.

Use catch words from the story to remind each other of the lesson: "Remember Casey and the cowboy 'stuff' on TV" may become your family's code for "remember to be thankful for what you have."

Young readers will enjoy reading the book to themselves and to their younger brothers and sisters. Nonreaders can tell themselves the story by looking at the pictures after it's been read aloud a couple of times.

Building Christian character is hard work—but it can be done in an enjoyable way, as *Casey the Greedy Young Cowboy* points out.

Cowboy Casey had a horse,
A purebred peddle-horse of course.
He raced it 'round the kitchen chairs
And galloped up the hallway stairs.

He trotted to the living room
To watch his favorite noon cartoon.
His favorite show was *Cowboy Days*,
He watched it while his horsey grazed.

And as he watched his cowboy show
With bucking broncs and rodeos,
Cowboy Casey had a thought—
"Hey! They've got stuff I haven't GOT!
All those cowboys on TV
Have more cowboy stuff than me!"

7

So, Cowboy Casey wrote a list,
He wrote so long he strained his wrist!

Stuff I Need he wrote on top,
And then he ran to Mom and Pop.

8

"Here," said Casey, "here's a list.
I need this stuff, I must insist!
Every cowboy on TV
Has this stuff . . . but not poor me!"

His mom and dad were pretty shocked,
A long time passed before they talked.
"This list is rather long," said Dad.
"You're sure you need these things real bad?"

Cowboy Casey nodded, "Yes."
And said, "Make sure you get the best!"

"Now, Casey," Mom said with a frown.
"I think that you should look around.
We've bought you cowboy hats and boots,
Silver stars and two six-shoots.
But more than that, you shouldn't groan—
You have a family, friends, a home!"

That made Casey very mad—
Very mad at Mom and Dad!
He jumped upon his horse's back
And stormed outside—the door went SMACK!

12

He rolled his peddle-horse along,
Humming angry cowboy songs.
But as he muttered at the sky,
Something near him caught his eye—

First Baptist Church
MEDIA LIBRARY

13

A poster for a rodeo!
A rodeo! What do you know!
With cowboys, hot dogs, bulls, and clowns—
Coming soon to Casey's town!

Cowboy Casey snatched the sign
And peddled home in little time.
Forgetting that he'd been so mad,
He showed the sign to Mom and Dad.
"Sure," they said, "we'd love to go—
We'll take you to the rodeo!"

The rodeo was big and loud.
What a show! And what a crowd!
They rode on bulls and broncos, too,
It was like a dream come true!

And then there came a big surprise . . .
A cowboy who was Casey's size!

Casey watched the boy and thought,
"What a swell life that kid's got!
His parents must be really great. . . .
I'll bet that he's not even eight!"

The boy, whose name was Bronco Bill,
Had a trailer on a hill.
Casey watched Bill go inside,
And then he took a little ride.

19

He went and knocked on Bill's front door. . . .
No answer . . . so he knocked once more.

He opened it, and looked around.
Then he heard a sobbing sound—
And there, in tears, was Bronco Bill
Leaning on the windowsill.

"Oh, my!" said Casey. "Are you hurt?
Did you get shot by Black-eyed Bert?"

"No," sobbed Bill, "I just feel sad.
I wish I had a mom and dad.
I live here all alone, you see,
'Cause I don't have a family!"

"You mean that's *all*?" said Casey doubting.
"That's no reason to be pouting!
You've got everything you need—
Bulls and guns and broncs with speed!"

"Sure," said Bill, "but I'm alone.
Would you want this for a home?
All the others in the show
Have a home, a place to go.
Look around. What do you see?
Is this a place you'd want to be?"

22

The place was small and dark and sad—
No pets, no friends, no Mom and Dad.
"How awfully lonely," Casey thought.
"I'd rather have the life I've got!"

23

It all came clear to Casey then—
How awfully thankless he had been. . . .
Thankless for the things he had,
Thankless for his mom and dad.
All this time he'd whined and moaned
While living in a happy home!

And as he hung his head in shame,
He heard a voice call out his name.
"Casey! Casey! Where are you?
It's time to go, the show is through."

Quickly Casey got a plan.
"Come on!" he cried, and took Bill's hand.

"Hey, Mom! Hey, Dad!" Casey screamed.
They turned and both their faces beamed!
"Casey, Son, where did you go?
You had us worried sick, you know!"

"Meet my new pal, Bronco Bill,
He lives alone up on the hill.
He's even in the rodeo. . . .
He's the best one in the show!

"And he's got tons of cowboy stuff,
But I found out that's not enough.
You see, he has no Mom or Dad. . . .
And that's why Bronco Bill's so sad.

"He really shouldn't be alone. . . .
Don't you think he needs a home?
I could sort of be his brother—
You could be his dad and mother!
'Cause you're the greatest, Mom and Dad—
And having you sure makes me glad!"

Cowboy Casey's parents smiled
And hugged their little cowboy child.
They hugged his new friend Billy, too—
This thankfulness was something new!

Give thanks to the Lord, for He is good; For His lovingkindness is everlasting.

Psalm 118:1 (NASB)

Look for all the great stories in the
Building Christian Character series

Buzzle Billy—A Book About Sharing
Handy-Dandy Helpful Hal—A Book About Helpfulness
Miggy and Tiggy—A Book About Overcoming Jealousy
Suzy Swoof—A Book About Kindness
Max and the Big Fat Lie—A Book About Telling the Truth
Casey the Greedy Young Cowboy—A Book About Being Thankful
Sir Maggie the Mighty—A Book About Obedience
Boggin, Blizzy, and Sleeter the Cheater—A Book About Fairness